DR XARGLE'S
—— BOOK OF ——
EARTHLETS

1 3 5 7 9 10 8 6 4 2

Text © 1988 Jeanne Willis
Illustrations © 1988 Tony Ross

Jeanne Willis and Tony Ross have asserted their rights under
the Copyright, Designs and Patents Act, 1988
to be identified as author and illustrator of this work

First published in the United Kingdom 1988
by Andersen Press
First published in Mini Treasures edition 1996
by Red Fox
Random House, 20 Vauxhall Bridge Road, London SW1V 2SA

Random House Australia (Pty) Limited
20 Alfred Street, Milsons Point, Sydney,
New South Wales 2061, Australia

Random House New Zealand Limited
18 Poland Road, Glenfield,
Auckland 10, New Zealand

Random House South Africa (Pty) Limited
PO Box 2263, Rosebank 2121, South Africa

Random House UK Limited Reg. No. 954009

A CIP catalogue record for this book
is available from the British Library

ISBN 009 9725 517

Printed in Singapore

JEANNE WILLIS & TONY ROSS

DR XARGLE'S
── BOOK OF ──
EARTHLETS

Mini Treasures
RED FOX

Good morning, class.

Today we are going to learn about Earthlets.

They come in four colours. Pink, brown, black or yellow ... but not green.

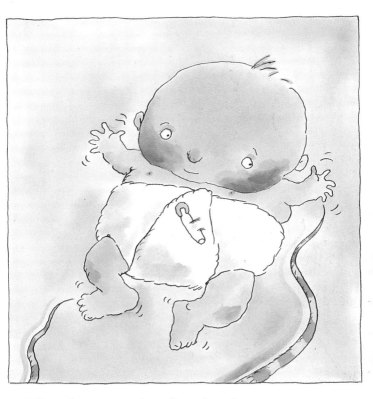

They have one head and only two eyes, two short tentacles with pheelers on the end and two long tentacles called leggies.

They have square claws which they use to frighten off wild beasts known as Tibbles and Marmaduke.

Earthlets grow fur on their heads but not enough to keep them warm.

They must be wrapped in the hairdo of a sheep.

Very old Earthlings (or 'Grannies') unravel the sheep and with two pointed sticks they make Earthlet wrappers in blue and white and pink.

Earthlets have no fangs at birth.
For many days they drink only milk through
a hole in their face.

When they have finished the milk they must be patted and squeezed to stop them exploding.

When they grow a fang, the parent
Earthling takes the egg of a hen and
mangles it with a prong.

Then she puts the eggmangle on a small spade and tips it into the Earthlet's mouth, nose and ears.

To stop them leaking, Earthlets must be
pulled up by the back tentacles and folded in
half. Then they must be wrapped quickly in a
fluffy triangle or sealed with paper and glue.

During the day, Earthlets collect the hairs
of Tibbles and Marmaduke, mud,
eggmangle and banana.

They are then placed in plastic capsules
with warm water and a yellow floating bird.

After soaking, Earthlets must be dried
carefully to stop them shrinking.
Then they are sprinkled with dust to stop
them sticking to things.

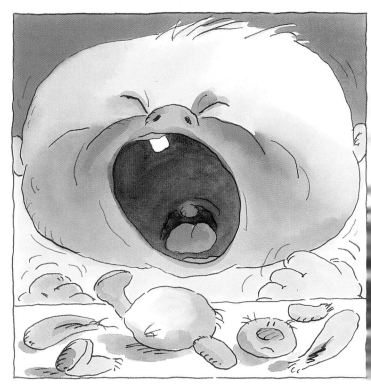

Earthlets can be recognised by their fierce
cry, 'WAAAAAAA!'

To stop them doing this, the Earthling
daddy picks them up and flings them into
the atmosphere.

Then he tries to catch them.

If they still cry, the Earthling mummy pulls
their pheelers one by one and says 'This
little piggy went to market' until the
Earthlet makes a 'hee hee' noise.

If they still cry, they are sent to a place called beddybyes.

This is a swinging box with a soft lining in which there lives a small bear called Teddy.

That is the end of today's lesson.

If you are all very good and quiet we are
going to put our disguises on and visit
planet Earth to see some real Earthlets.

The spaceship leaves in five minutes.